AND TWO BOYS BOOED

JUDITH VIORST

Pictures by

SOPHIE BLACKALL

MARGARET FERGUSON BOOKS
Farrar Straus Giroux
New York

For Olivia Rigel Viorst, of course!

–J.V.

For Olive, Eggy, Jack, and Bea

–S.B.

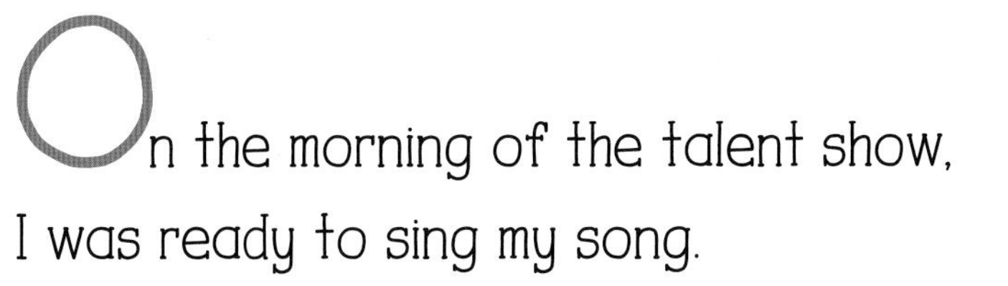

On the morning of the talent show,
I was ready to sing my song.

La-la-la
La-la-la
La-la-la
La-la-la
La-la-la
Mmphl-mmfl
La-la-la
La-la-la
La-la-la
La-la-la
La-la-la
La-la-la
La-la-la
La-la-la
La-la-la
La-la-la

And I wasn't one bit scared because I had practiced a billion times,

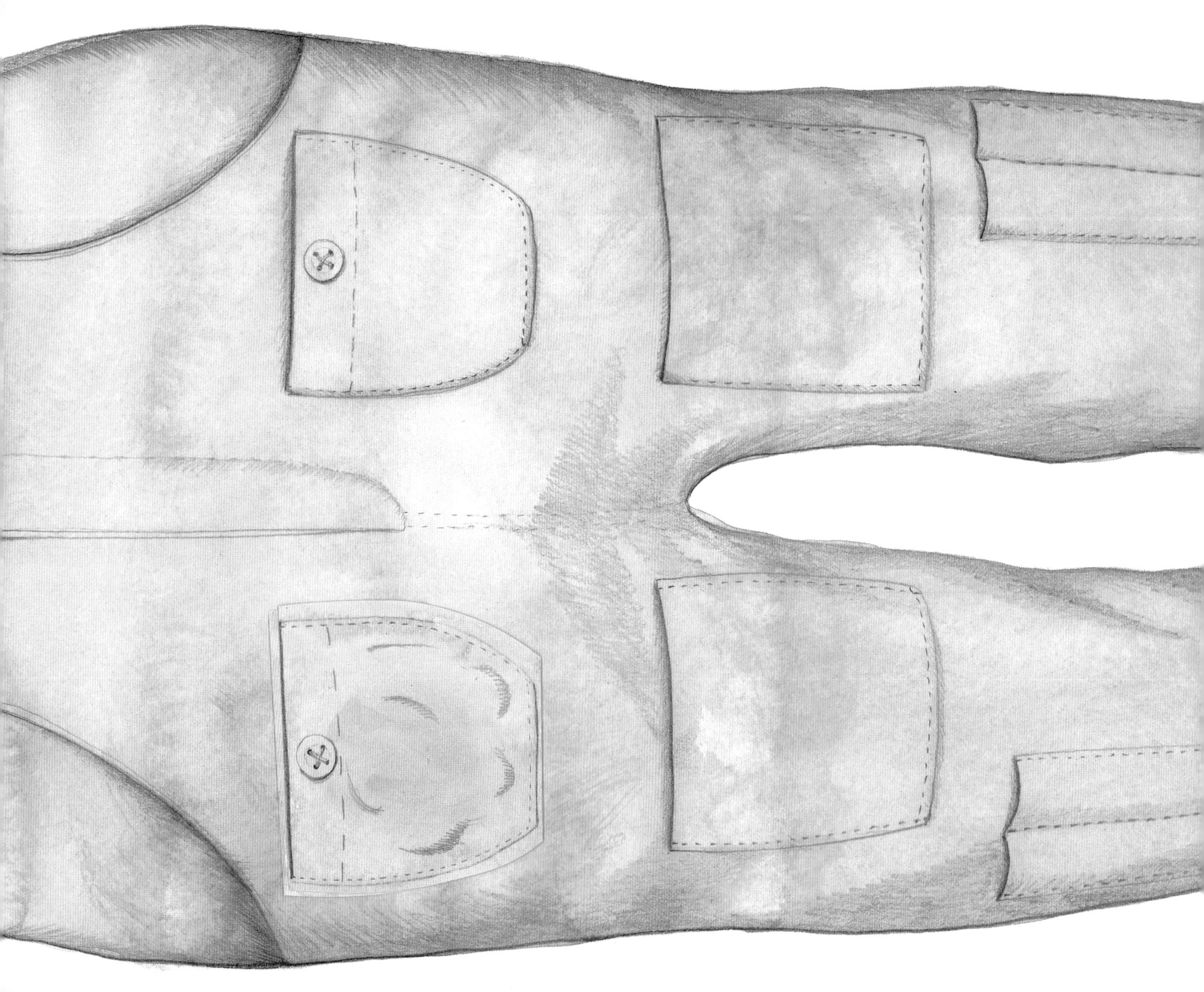

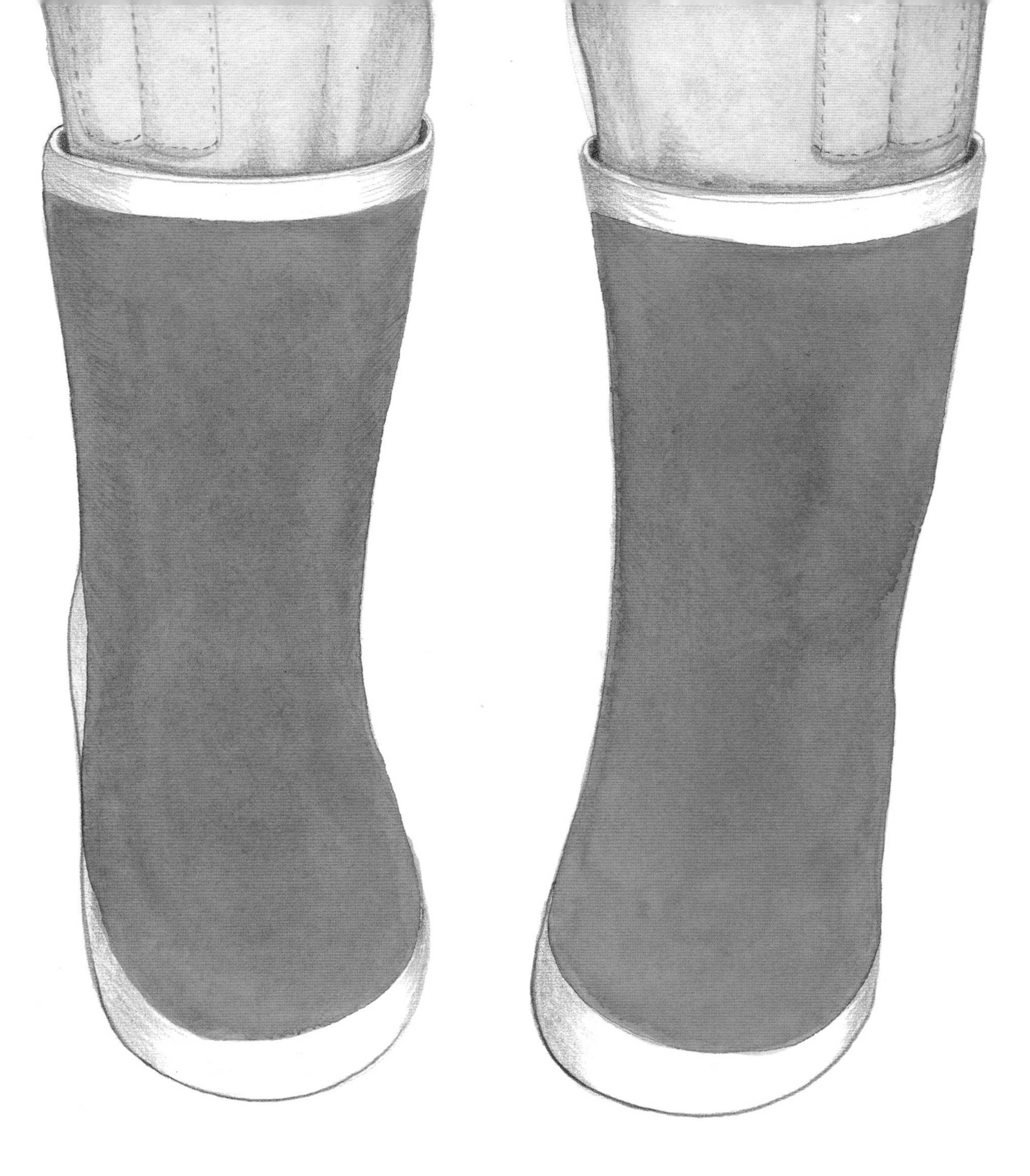

plus I was wearing my lucky blue boots
and my pants with cool pockets.

There were five other kids in the show,

and then there was me.

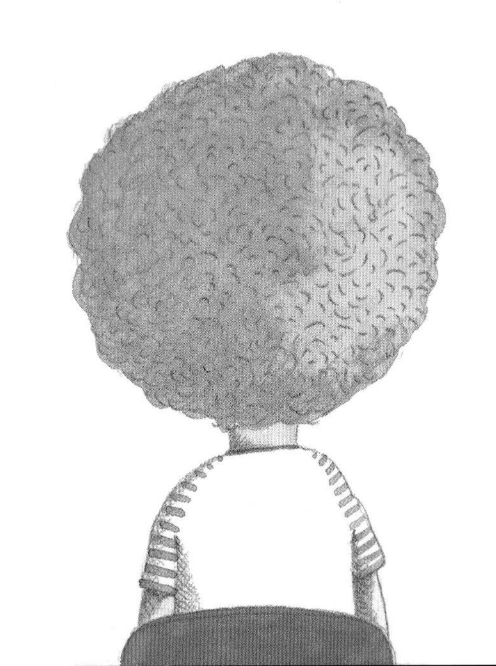

On the morning of the talent show,
I was ready to sing my song.
And I wasn't one bit scared because I had practiced a billion times,
plus I was wearing my lucky blue boots and my pants with cool pockets.
But after Chloe had read her poem,
there were four other kids left to go,
and then there was me.

On the morning of the talent show,
I was ready to sing my song.
And I wasn't one bit scared because I had practiced a billion times,
plus I was wearing my lucky blue boots and my pants with cool pockets.
But after Chloe had read her poem,
and after Henry had walked on his hands,
there were three other kids left to go,
and then there was me.

On the morning of the talent show,
I was ready to sing my song.
And I wasn't one bit scared because I had practiced a billion times,
plus I was wearing my lucky blue boots and my pants with cool pockets.
But after Chloe had read her poem,
and after Henry had walked on his hands,
and after Georgia had danced on her toes,
there were two other kids left to go,
and then there was me.

On the morning of the talent show,
I was ready to sing my song.
And I wasn't one bit scared because I had practiced a billion times,
plus I was wearing my lucky blue boots and my pants with cool pockets.
But after Chloe had read her poem,
and after Henry had walked on his hands,
and after Georgia had danced on her toes,
and after Leo had juggled some balls,
there was one other kid left to go,
and then there was me.

On the morning of the talent show,
I was ready to sing my song.
And I wasn't one bit scared because I had practiced a billion times,
plus I was wearing my lucky blue boots and my pants with cool pockets.
But after Chloe had read her poem,
and after Henry had walked on his hands,
and after Georgia had danced on her toes,
and after Leo had juggled some balls,
and after Madeleine had shown us the pictures she painted,
there were no other kids left to go.
There was just me.

On the **talent** of the **morning** show,
I was ready to **song** my **sing**.
And I wasn't one bit scared because I had practiced a billion times,
plus I was wearing my lucky blue **pants** and my **boots** with cool pockets.
But after Chloe had read her poem,
and after Henry had walked on his hands,
and after Georgia had danced on her toes,
and after Leo had juggled some balls,
and after Madeleine had shown us
the pictures she painted,
there were no other kids left to go.
So I stood in **class** of our **front**.
I just stood there,
and then I sat down.
And then I got up.
And then I sat down.
And two boys booed.

Boo
Boo

On the **talent** of the **morning** show,
I was ready to **song** my **sing**.
And I maybe was one bit scared although I had practiced a billion times,
plus I was wearing my lucky blue **pants** and my **boots** with cool pockets.
There were no other kids left to go,
so I stood in **class** of our **front**.
I just stood there,
and then I sat down.
And then I got up.
And then I sat down.
And after I got up and sat down and got up and sat down some more,
because I kept changing my mind about **songing** my **sing**,

I started **walking** my **poem**.

I mean, I started **dancing** my **hands**.

I mean, I started **reading** my **toes**.

I mean, I started **painting** some **balls**.

I mean, I started **juggling** the **pictures** I had shown me.

I mean, I started singing my song.

And two boys booed.

But all the other kids were clapping!

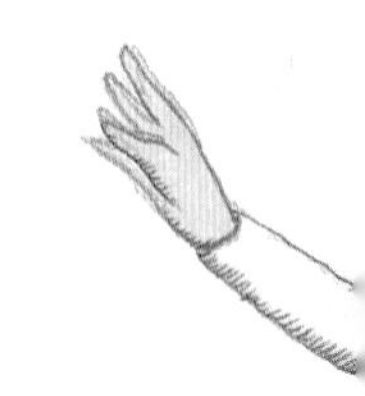

Farrar Straus Giroux Books for Young Readers
175 Fifth Avenue, New York 10010

Color separations by Bright Arts (H.K.) Ltd.
Printed in China by South China Printing Co. Ltd.,
Dongguan City, Guangdong Province
Designed by Roberta Pressel
First edition, 2014
10 9 8 7 6 5 4 3 2 1

mackids.com

Library of Congress Cataloging-in-Publication Data
Viorst, Judith.
And two boys booed / Judith Viorst ; pictures by Sophie Blackall.—
First edition.
pages cm
Summary: A boy is nervous about a presentation he has to give at school.
ISBN 978-0-374-30302-0 (hardcover)
[1. Fear—Fiction. 2. Stage fright—Fiction.] I. Blackall, Sophie, illustrator.
II. Title.
PZ7.V816Ao 2914
[E]—dc23
2013007871

Farrar Straus Giroux Books for Young Readers may be purchased
for business or promotional use. For information on bulk purchases
please contact Macmillan Corporate and Premium Sales Department
at (800) 221-7945 x5442 or by email at specialmarkets@macmillan.com.